The Woolly Jumper

ISBN 978-0-9564515-0-7

Published in the UK in 2009 by
Award Design and Print   email: cedricwilson@live.co.uk

If

you were to
drive along
the Ballywiggle Road
just past the big puddle...

you would see at Knitmore Farm a big field full of sheep.

If you could count them there would be one hundred.

They all
looked the same,
spoke the same,
and
liked
the same food.

Farmer Trulove called them his
Woolly Jumpers;

but
one sheep
was not
very happy,

he was
bored.

He wanted to
go somewhere nice
and do something new.

One afternoon
two boys
zoomed past on
skateboards,

"That looks **fun**," thought the woolly jumper.

They did jumps and **tricks**.

But one
of the
boys

fell and hurt himself

As he fell
he broke
the wheel
on his
skateboard.

He was cross,
he threw it
over the hedge
and limped home.

"I could
fix that,"

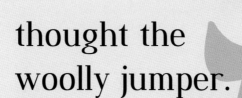

thought the
woolly jumper.

So he did!

Ninety nine sheep
sat in the field
but one was skateboarding.

"You are going to
get into trouble,"
said one of the sheep.

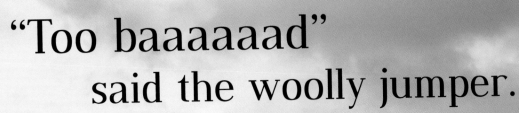

He made a ramp
so he could jump
higher.

"I think I could
jump that hedge,"
said the woolly jumper -

so he did!

Then he began to
ask himself
things like

"What's over the
next hedge?" ...

... "where does that path go?"

"Is the grass greener over there?"

Then he began to **worry**.

"It's getting late and I am getting hungry."

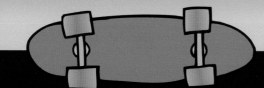

Ninety nine sheep
sat in the field
but
something was wrong.

They could not
settle for bed

Farmer Trulove counted them and one was missing.

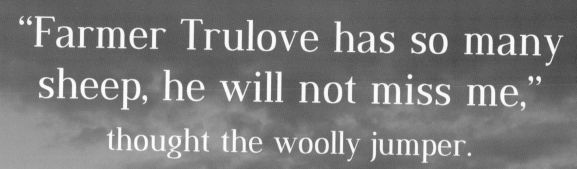

"Farmer Trulove has so many sheep, he will not miss me," thought the woolly jumper.

But he *was missed*
and he *was loved*
He *was just as special* as the
other ninety nine sheep.

The book you have been reading was
based on a story told by the Lord Jesus.
You can read it in the Bible.

(Luke Chapter 15; verses 3-7)

Think about this:

Everyone is important to God.
He wants us to believe and trust in Him.
We break His heart when we do wrong. He loved us so much He
allowed His Son Jesus to take the blame and be punished instead of us.
He would be so happy to see you in heaven some day.

Are you going the right way or are you lost?
Jesus said:
I am the Way the Truth and the Life.